W9-ALV-501

Dear Parents:

Congratulations! Your child is taking the first steps on an exciting journey. The destination? Independent reading!

STEP INTO READING® will help your child get there. The program offers five steps to reading success. Each step includes fun stories and colorful art or photographs. In addition to original fiction and books with favorite characters, there are Step into Reading Non-Fiction Readers, Phonics Readers and Boxed Sets, Sticker Readers, and Comic Readers—a complete literacy program with something to interest every child.

Learning to Read, Step by Step!

Ready to Read   Preschool–Kindergarten
• big type and easy words • rhyme and rhythm • picture clues
For children who know the alphabet and are eager to begin reading.

Reading with Help   Preschool–Grade 1
• basic vocabulary • short sentences • simple stories
For children who recognize familiar words and sound out new words with help.

Reading on Your Own   Grades 1–3
• engaging characters • easy-to-follow plots • popular topics
For children who are ready to read on their own.

Reading Paragraphs   Grades 2–3
• challenging vocabulary • short paragraphs • exciting stories
For newly independent readers who read simple sentences with confidence.

Ready for Chapters   Grades 2–4
• chapters • longer paragraphs • full-color art
For children who want to take the plunge into chapter books but still like colorful pictures.

STEP INTO READING® is designed to give every child a successful reading experience. The grade levels are only guides; children will progress through the steps at their own speed, developing confidence in their reading.

Remember, a lifetime love of reading starts with a single step!

Thomas the Tank Engine & Friends™

CREATED BY BRITT ALLCROFT

Based on The Railway Series by The Reverend W Awdry.
© 2015 Gullane (Thomas) LLC.
Thomas the Tank Engine & Friends and Thomas & Friends are trademarks of Gullane
(Thomas) Limited.
HIT and the HIT Entertainment logo are trademarks of HIT Entertainment Limited.

This work is based on *Valentine's Day in Vicarstown,* originally published by Random House
Children's Books in 2008. Copyright © 2008 Gullane (Thomas) LLC.

Visit us on the Web!
StepIntoReading.com
randomhousekids.com
www.thomasandfriends.com

Educators and librarians, for a variety of teaching tools, visit us at
RHTeachersLibrarians.com

ISBN 978-1-101-93287-2 (trade) — ISBN 978-1-101-93288-9 (lib. bdg.) —
ISBN 978-1-101-93289-6 (ebook)

Printed in the United States of America
10 9 8 7 6 5 4 3 2 1

HIT entertainment

THOMAS & FRIENDS™

A Valentine for Percy

Based on The Railway Series
by The Reverend W Awdry

Illustrated by Richard Courtney

Random House 🏠 New York

It was almost
Valentine's Day.
Thomas had to work
away from the Sheds.

He said goodbye to
Percy.

On Valentine's Day,
it snowed!

Percy could not

see very well!

Percy waited
for Thomas to plow.

Thomas was too far
away.

Sir Topham Hatt
asked Percy to plow!

Percy used

Thomas' plow.

He helped clear
away the snow.

Percy even

delivered the mail.

It was time
for the Valentine party.

Percy saw the mailboxes.
He hoped he would
get a valentine.

Sir Topham Hatt
greeted everyone.

The children sang.

Percy said hello
to the children.

The children put
valentines in the
boxes.

It was time

to count the valentines.

Percy got the most!

The last card
was from Thomas.

"Thank you for plowing
the snow,"
he said.

It was Percy's

favorite valentine!